Oh, That Cat!

Norma Simon
pictures by Dora Leder

ALBERT WHITMAN & COMPANY, MORTON GROVE, ILLINOIS

Library of Congress Cataloging-in-Publication Data

Simon, Norma.
  Oh, that cat!

  Summary: Max the cat can be a real pain or very
nice, but his owners love him better than any cat in
the world.
  [1. Cats—Fiction.] I. Leder, Dora, ill. II. Title.
PZ7.S6053Oh   1986   [E]   85-15546
ISBN 0-8075-5919-9 (lib. bdg.)

The text of this book is printed in sixteen-point Caslon 540.

In the middle of the night,
my cat pounces on me.

"OUUUU-T!" he meows, over and over,
until I get out of bed,
and ouuuu-t goes Max.

When Max wants to come back,
he makes Mom and Dad mad.
He licks his front paws
and squeaks them across the glass.

"SCRITCHCHCHCHCH!"
until somebody lets him in.

Oh, that cat!

Everyone in my family has work to do,
but not my cat.

He does what he likes all day long.

He climbs inside my bunny slippers.

He hides inside the hamper.

He jumps in the bathtub with me.

He sits on a chair
licking his belly
like a big, fat raccoon.

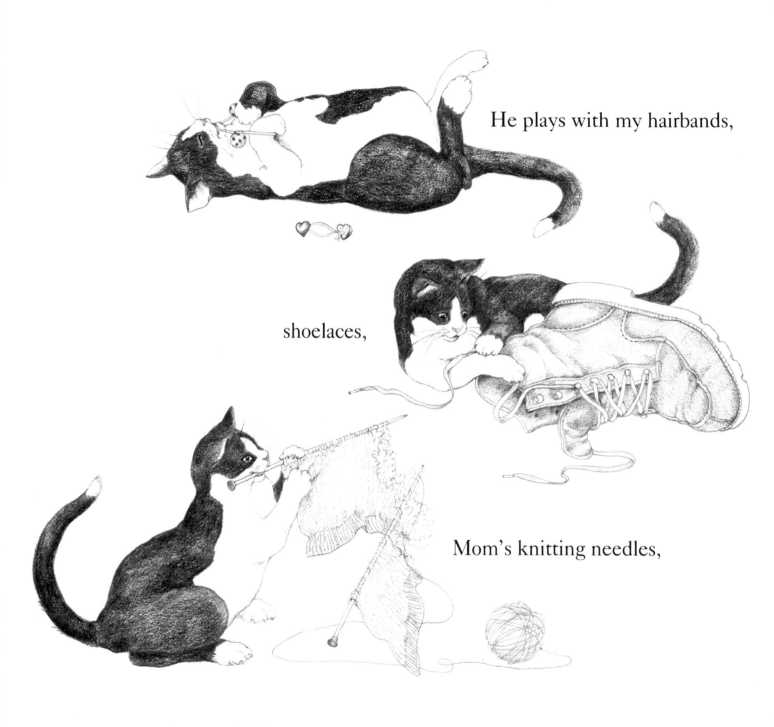

He plays with my hairbands,

shoelaces,

Mom's knitting needles,

moths,

shadows,

and his own tail.

He thinks everything in the world is just for him.

We eat when it's eating time,
but not Max!
He eats whenever he feels like it.
Then he hangs around the refrigerator,
begging for more.

Or he gets up on my lap
and tries to eat off my dish.

Oh, that cat!

We've all been mad at Max
for different things he does.

Mom got mad
when Max dug up her zucchini seeds.

Dad got mad when he petted Max,
and Max turned around and scratched him.

Grandpa got mad
when Max knocked over his adding machine.

Grandma got mad
when a skunk sprayed Max,
and she had to shampoo him
with tomato juice.
Yuck! What a mess!

(But it wasn't really his fault.)

And when Max climbed up our Christmas tree
and almost knocked it down,
we all yelled at him.

OH, THAT CAT!

But I love it when Max
rubs his head on my legs
and purrs very loud
until I scratch his head.

Or when he sleeps on my feet.
(He's my own private heater.)

I like to watch him

climb

and jump

and flip.

I like it when he makes everyone laugh.

Sometimes we go for walks.

And sometimes he plays hide-and-seek with me
when I don't have anyone else to play with.

One night Max went away.
He didn't come back for a long time.
I called him,
and I looked for him
everywhere.

When Max came home,
I hugged him and I squeezed him hard.

Oh, that cat!